THE MAGICAL NURSE

Dan DL Smith

Dedicated to my little sister, Kacey

A NEW PATIENT

Jasmine bursts through the door of the children's ward lying flat on a hospital bed. Tears rolling down her bright red face. Pain extruding from every part of her body. Every bone frozen from fear from the last few hours. A folder is passed between the porter and a nurse, who had greeted the group upon arrival. Jasmine clenches Flopsy (her grey Mini Lop Rabbit teddy) close to her chest, burying her head into the ears of the teddy. Half her face hidden either by the teddy's ears or her thick, curly black hair. Her Mother and Father stay close to each side of the bed, anxiously awaiting the nurses' next move.

"Hello there!" The nurse greeted Jasmine with a warming smile. "What's your name?" Jasmine looks up at the soothing face that confronted her at the bottom of the bed.

"Jasmine." She replied after hesitation.

"Good afternoon, Jasmine! My name is Fiona, and I'll be looking after you! We have a special room ready just for you." She places the folder at the reception desk and leads Jasmine's bed forward through the corridor. An army of nurses and porters protecting all sides of the bed. Lights lit the never-ending hallway brightly causing Jasmine to shield her eyes even more. Large characters stretching the height of the walls were painted between each door. The entourage stopped after about ten doors. They turned the bed around the corner and into a small room.

The walls of the room were sunshine yellow with magical characters lining the walls, each dancing along to musical notes surrounding them. Two light wooden armchairs sat on each side of a small window opposite the door, both drenched in a thick red velvet cloth. Underneath the window stood a small box laced with glitter, bursting with books and toys. Fiona placed Jasmine's bed in the centre of the room before pushing the bed back towards the plug sockets on the wall. The bed now rest against the wall, between two chairs and a small table.

"This is your room. You have a whole room to yourself for now." Fiona stated. "If you need anything, make sure you push this bright orange button, and I'll be right back." Fiona leaves the call button by Jasmine's side and quietly steps away. Turning to Mum and Dad before leaving the room, "A Doctor will be around soon with a further diagnosis on her situation."

Jasmine turns her head from her rabbit ear shield and towards her mother; who is by her side. "Mummy. I'm scared."

Mother leans in for an enormous hug while Jasmine reaches out. Kind words of support are shared by both parents followed by a harrowing silence. A few moments later, a doctor walks into the room. He is a tall, middle-aged fellow with thick-rimmed glasses and a smartly shaved beard. His attire was suggestive that he's not one for surgery, and would rather have a clipboard on him at all times instead.

"Avon and Leo Gould, I presume?" He announced in his soft yet uniformly concerned voice. Mother and Father greet him with a nod. The doctor walks further into the room. "And this must be little Jasmine. How old are you, Jasmine?" The doctor asks. After a little hesitation, and an encouraging nudge from her Mother, she replies "Six... And a half."

"Ah!" Replies the doctor. "My name is Dr Richmond, and I'll be here to find out how we can make you all better again so you can go home. Sound good?"

Jasmine nodded, once again grabbing Flopsy and holding him close. "Mr and Mrs Gould. May we have this word outside?". The three adults leave the room, shutting the door behind them. Jasmine hugs Flopsy even tighter, pulling him closer to her chest and turning on her side towards the window. She closes her eyes tight, trying not to let the pain affect her.

Suddenly, there's a single knock at the window. Jasmine sharply opens her eyes. She stares out of the window, startled. Nothing has moved. She keeps staring at the window, holding her breath. A faint purple glow illuminates the very bottom of the glass, causing the room to light a subtle purple as it reflects off the window ledge. Jasmine hears a muffled human-sounding whistle radiating from the light source. The door behind Jasmine bursts open, and the light promptly disappears. Her Mother and Father re-entered the room, both taking a seat in the armchairs near Jasmine. Both parents put on brave faces, but Jasmine could tell something was wrong. Very wrong. Once again, tears began to roll down Jasmine's face and soaking Flopsy on their descent as she spoke softly.

"Am I going to die?"

Jasmine's mum bounced up from her armchair and sat on the bed, continuing to comfort her. "Of course not, sweetheart. You're safe here. We'll get through this together, don't worry, sweetheart."

Leo, on the other hand, stayed eerily silent; Lost in contemplation. It only took a few seconds for Leo to start pacing the room. Back and forth, back and forth, back and forth.

"Leo, stop that!" Avon demanded, switching her attention away from Jasmine just for a second. Her fiery stare prompts Leo to be seated once more. Leo throws himself down upon the armchair once more, crossing his arms and his legs. Avon continues to stroke Jasmine's head, gently moving her coiled hair away from her face as Jasmine's eyes get heavy.
"Mummy. I feel sleepy."
"That's okay, darling. Try to get some sleep."
Jasmine's eyes continue to get heavier, slowly shutting before darting back open again. Jasmine tries to persist. Eventually, Jasmine falls into a dream, closing her eyes peacefully.

THE NURSE

A few hours later, Jasmine wakes up. The sky out of the window had faded into the soft nighttime. Shadowy trees wave gently underneath the stars far above. A small fox pounces through the underbrush floors below, scouting the sun-deserted land for food. Jasmine opens her eyes to her mother quietly exiting the room.

"Mummy?"

Avon turns around and smiles. "I'll only be gone for a little while, sweetheart. Mummy just needs to make a phone call and get some coffee."

And with that, Jasmine is left alone. She gazes out of the window from the bed, lost in wonder about the twinkles in the sky. The gentle glow of the moon spreads a blanket of tranquillity across the land. All the day dwelling creatures settle down for the night. She notices one particular twinkle in the sky keeps flashing. Like it's saying 'Hello'.

"What a curious thing." Jasmine thought. "Maybe just an aeroplane? But it's not moving. It's glowing more orange than the red flashes of a plane..." Her thoughts are interrupted by the noise of the door squeaking open.

Standing in the doorway is a very jolly young adult, appearing to be another nurse at the hospital.

"Hi, Jasmine. How are you feeling?" She asked.

Jasmine looks around at the woman. Her hair is a light blonde with candy pink at the tips. Skin as pale as Ivory and her frame slender. Jasmine nodded to answer her question.

"You seem very lost in thought, young one. What could you be so curious about, I wonder."

Jasmine looks over at the sky and addresses the flashing star. The nurse walks over to the window, peeking outside into the night sky. She turns around and smiles back at Jasmine.

"That, my friend, is the star saying hello. Wishing you well. It's also saying hello to the floating gloflower outside of your window." The nurse explained. Her eyes starting to glow the same pink hue as the tips of her hair.

"A.. A Gloflower?" Jasmine was shocked. She'd never heard anything of a gloflower before. The nurse nods with excitement and turns back toward the window. She reaches out, softly bringing in a purple ball of light that floats just above her palm. Jasmine climbs out of bed to join the nurse. The nurse's hands resting gently on the window ledge.

"These are extraordinary creatures. Curiously energetic, might I add." Continued the nurse in a gentle tone; as if a secret is whispered. "They only show up when magic folk are worried or in need. So they're fairly common here, not so much anywhere else. Once you've made a wish, it travels north towards the northern lights to send the wish out. Here."

Jasmine reaches out of the window, holding her hands into a bowl shape. The Gloflower slowly drifts out of the nurse's hand and into Jasmines. Light from the Gloflower softly caresses Jasmine's face as she retracts her arms from the window. Jasmine holds the orb close to her chest. With her eyes closed, she whispers:
"I wish my family wasn't upset and stressed because of me."
Jasmines eyes opened slowly, and once again, the Gloflower begins to warm up. A soothing, gentle heat - as if Jasmine's hands were under a heat lamp. The warmth continued through her arms, soothing every muscle it travels past. Jasmine places her arms back onto the window ledge, allowing the Gloflower to send her to wish off. She took a deep breath and slowly unclasped her hands.

The gloflower jolts with a burst of energy; Shooting into the air! It rises around twenty metres before stopping dead in its tracks. The gloflower flickers and turns around as if it is calculating the direction like the GPS in Jasmine's Dad's car. Then it suddenly shoots off as swift as light, racing northbound. The nurse peers down at Jasmine, who's wide-eyed fascinated, smiling down while thinking to herself as she watches. The purple orb soon is only seen as a speck in the sky. Jasmine's fascination was short-lived as her eyes beginning to flood with tears once more.

The nurse looks over to the other side of the room and sharply reaches her hand out. A box of tissues flies across the room and into her hand. "Tissue?" The nurse offered. Jasmine takes a tissue to wipe her eyes, not noticing the existence of the tissue box. After Jasmine rubbed her eyes, she turned her head.
"Wow." Her eyes widen in astonishment as she notices the tissue box continuing to float in the air. The nurse leans over the window ledge, resting her arms while gazing up at the stars.

"Where I come from, Gloflowers are everywhere in the fields. It's where they go to rest once they've fulfilled their purpose. The whole field twinkles at night, almost like the stars. There are people like us there too. I hope you get to see it one day. It's a wonderful place!"

Jasmine turns her attention back towards the nurse. "People like us?"

"Yeah, like you and me."

Jasmine stares out at the stars too. "Where do you come from?"

The nurse glances over at Jasmine. "Charlinbourne." The nurse replied. "Just east of the Mystic River." Jasmine looks up sharply at the nurse. She could've sworn she had heard of the place before. Maybe in a book? Or even a dream? She thought perhaps she'd never get to see it if she's still unwell. Tears start to build up behind her eyes once more, urging her to take another tissue and climb back into bed. Jasmine lays in silence, lost in thought.

"Why are Mummy and Daddy so upset with me?" She asked the nurse, who had perched herself into a chair by the window. The box of tissues continues to float over her shoulder weightlessly.

"Well..." The nurse didn't know how to start. "I guess they're just worried because you're ill. They're not upset with you personally. Hey, sometimes, adults are silly like that."

"But... you're an adult." Jasmine looks down, reclaiming Flopsy the rabbit.

"Well, yes, I'm a grown-up. But not all grown-ups are adults. Some of us are still children at heart. Besides, adults can't do this!"

The nurse looks over to a couple of books that had fallen behind the box of toys. She nods her head backwards. Suddenly, a book floats up from behind the toybox. The book glides through the air, making its way over to Jasmine. It gently floats down on top of the covers in Jasmine's lap.

This particular book just happened to be Jasmine's favourite bedtime story. Her mother would be forever reading it at bedtime.

Looking at the night sky, it was pretty late, so a story was long overdue. The front cover slowly swung open, engaging Jasmine into the first words of her favourite story. As the nurse came over to sit by at the bedside, Jasmine had already begun reading the story aloud. At the end of the page, the nurse gestured for the page to turn, and so it did. The page floated up as if caught by a gentle summer breeze before resting on the other side of the seam.

"How'd you do that?" Jasmine asks, snapping out of the book and into a state of ore once again.
"I just believed I could." replies the nurse with a smile. The nurse and Jasmine continued to read the page. At the end of the next page, the nurse suggests Jasmine should try to turn the paper.
Jasmine gestures for the page to turn, just like the nurse had, but it didn't move. "Believe you can do it." The nurse says. "Just tell the page to turn."

Jasmine closes her eyes. "Turn the page." she thinks hard to herself, "Turn over." She reopens her eyes and takes a deep breath, then gestures. A brief swishing movement from right to left with two fingers extended; Hovering above the paper. It doesn't turn. Jasmine takes another deep breath and focuses her attention. "Turn over. Please turn over." She gestures again, this time slower and more cautious. To her surprise, the page slowly lifts. She gestures a flick, and the page followed, falling to the other side of the book; Unveiling the words on the next page. The book took about fifteen minutes to get through, with each magical page turn getting easier and easier to perform. By the end, Jasmine was an expert.
"I think it's time to put the story away and maybe get some sleep." The nurse says as the back cover concludes the story once more. Jasmine places the book to the side and gets out of bed, preparing to set the book by the window where it had first arisen.

"You know there's an easier way." The nurse said, her eyes filling with wonder; Glowing with fantasy. Jasmine held the book out on the palm of her hands as the nurse stares profoundly. The book slowly starts to elevate from Jasmine's hands and float weightlessly in the air.

"Point to where you want it to go." The nurse instructs. Jasmine points in a direction, but the book remains still, as though it was already perched on an invisible table.

"Remember, Believe." Jasmine closes her eyes; "Move book. Go to your spot. Please move." Her eyes open and the intensity of her eyes lifted. Her pupils shrink thin, and her focus remains solely on the book. The book slowly continues to lift in the air. The book shakes a little as it stabilised itself against gravity. It then begins to move over the bed and the nurses head. Jasmine starts jumping and clapping at what she could do. The book falls to the ground.

"What happened?" Jasmine asks - now confused and incredibly disappointed with herself.

"You looked away." The nurse replies. "Here, like this." The nurse looks at the book as it starts to lift back off the ground. She gestures, flicking the book over towards the window. The book shoots over, stopping as suddenly as it starts, moving directly to the toy box. The nurse gives a great nod at the book, making it fall right on top of the toy box. "See. Focus and Believe. With those things, you can do anything! Now, you should try to get some rest little one. You are ill after all."

Jasmine smiles and lays back on the bed. The covers are tucked underneath her, while Flopsy perches by her head.

"Sleep well." The nurse says softly. Her voice was angelic, relaxing every muscle in Jasmine's body into a state of bliss. She clicks her fingers, the lights fade. And with that, she quietly steps out, leaving Jasmine to get some rest.

As tired and relaxed as Jasmine was, she couldn't sleep. The pain starts erupting in her stomach once more, and all she wanted to do was take her mind off it. Jasmine sits back up and clicks her fingers; Nothing happens. She clicks her fingers once more... Still nothing. It takes a few attempts but, eventually, the lights fill the room with light, making Jasmine jump. She hesitates before clicking again, trying to keep focus. Jasmine clicks her fingers; The lights go off. One more click. The lights flood the room with light once more. Jasmine smiles; She's starting to get the hang of this!

She looks around the room for something to practice moving. Jasmine notices the tissue box was still hovering by the chair. Focusing her eyes on the tissue box, Jasmine holds her breath. Her hands rise to point at the tissues; Drawing their trajectory in the air. The box shakes a little. Suddenly, it follows the gesture of Jasmine's hand. She gently moves her hand across her and points to the shelf on the other side of the room. The tissue box shoots across the room and hovers over the shelf. Jasmine gives the tissues a nod. They fall elegantly onto the shelf.

The door opens, and Avon, Jasmine's Mother, walks in, followed by a doctor. Jasmine quickly lays back down in bed and shuts her eyes. No one notices Jasmine is still awake.
"We'll take her to the theatre in the morning, and we'll fix the issues. I'm afraid there is not much we can do until then." The doctor explains. Avon nods in agreement, and the doctor dismisses himself. She sits down on one of the armchairs.
"Mum, why Am I going to theatre?" Jasmine asks, sitting back up in her bed.

Avon looks up. "They're going to fix you, sweetheart. Don't worry. You'll be better before you know it."
"What if I don't get better, Mum."
There is a profound silence. Avon has no words. Her eyes start to tear up. "Maybe we should try to get some sleep, Darling." Avon

stands back up to turn the lights off. Jasmine smiles mischievously and stares at the light switch. She clicks her fingers. Snap. The lights turn off.

"Oh," Avon is dumbfounded. She shrugs it off very quickly, however. "Must be on a timer. It is fairly late after all." Avon makes her way back to her seat as Jasmine's eyes close.

PIXEL

The following two hours felt like a second to Jasmine. "I must've fallen asleep pretty quickly." She thinks as she awakes again. The room is dark and silent. Even the rooms outside are dark and still; Af if they were trapped in time. Jasmine glances over at her Mother; Fast asleep in the armchair. Flopsy rabbit lay by her side. Jasmine puts her arms around Flopsy and squeezes him. "I hope I'm going to be okay." She murmurs into one of the floppy's ears. Her attention was distracted to the window as a soft orange light protruding from outside. Jasmine softly stands up, holding flopsy by the paw as she tip-toes to the window. The window was still open from earlier in the night.

"Gloflower?" Jasmine whispers into the cold night air, "Is that you?" A twinkling sound arises from the left side of the window. Tiny wind chimes can be heard swaying in the soft summer breeze. Jasmine looks towards the sound. A pixie around 6 inches tall was curled up at the side of the window, illuminating a warm orange glow.

"Hello there." Jasmine greets the creature. The pixie looks up, her glow fading to yellow as she shuffles away from Jasmine. "It's okay; I won't hurt you. You look awfully cold out there." The pixie looks up again; Nodding. Her glow fades to a frost-bitten blue. "Why don't you come in! I could do with the company." Jasmine invites the pixie inside.

The pixie stands up. She brushes herself down. Dust, dirt, and pixie glitter from the window ledge had accumulated on her dress. The dress was coloured in rainbow sequins down to her knees, with bright white tights and a little headband. A tiny gold necklace with 'P' on the pendant rests around her neck. Her wings flutter as she moves through the window; Perching herself on Jasmine's shoulder. Jasmine walks back to the bed and sits cross-legged in the centre with Flopsy in front of her. "What's your name?" Jasmine asked. The pixie flies to hover in front of Jasmine, drawing a dot in floating, glowing dust. She smiles.

"Dot?" Jasmine questions. "Is that your name?"

The pixie shook her head. She pointed to herself.

"Umm... Fairy?" Jasmine continues, trying to guess the pixies name as if it were a game of charades. The pixie rolled her eyes and sighed.

"Oh! Pixie!" The pixie wiggles her toes with excitement; Jasmine was getting close! The creature draws an 'L' with the dust from the dot, rendering Jasmine confused.

"Uh... La Pixie?" The pixie sank as she crosses her arms in dispute.

"I don't know" Jasmine sighs. The pixie points furiously at the letter 'L' hovering in the air.

Jasmine starts to think of what the creatures name could be. She was never good with Charades, even at the best of times. Then it

Clicked!

"Pixel!" Jasmine smiles excitedly. The pixie jumps back up; Her glow changing lime green. She bursts into a huge smile and a thumbs up!

"Hi Pixel, I'm Jasmine!" Pixel sighs, giving off the sound of wind chimes. Her movements accidentally move the dust in the air. The glittery dust floats toward Jasmine, making her sneeze. Pixel swerves and dodges the multiple torpedoes of snot and dust extruding from Jasmine's nose. Jasmine reaches out for the tissue box. The box effortlessly rises from the shelf and shoots right into Jasmine's hands like a magnet; Almost hitting Pixel once more.

After Jasmine's sneezing fit came to a close, she apologises to Pixel, who was perched back on her knee; Not very impressed.

"Should I be asleep? To rest for tomorrow?" Jasmine asks. Pixel nods. Jasmine sighs. "But I keep waking up. Ugh, I really hate hospitals." She
continued.

Pixel starts thinking. Then Eureka! She jumps up and flies to the top of Jasmine's head and shakes. Multicoloured dust flutters from her dress and into Jasmine's hair like a waterfall of glitter, making Jasmine sleepy. After a few seconds, Jasmine falls backwards fast asleep cross-legged on top of the covers; Just like being knocked out by a sedative.

Pixel flies back down onto Jasmine's leg, wiping her hands clean from a job well done. Her glow turns a bright, warming glow of confidence as she flicks her golden hair out and proudly walks down Jasmine's leg. Suddenly, there's an loud thump. Pixel jumps, turning yellow as she crouches into a ball. Something starts sniffing above her. Little did she realise that the dust didn't just land on Jasmine. The dust had landed on Flopsy as well, making the rabbit come alive! A giant rabbit now towers over Pixel with huge sniffling puffs of air, making Pixels hair windswept.

Flopsy reaches out with one of his front paws towards Pixel as she dodges and flies directly upwards. She hovers above Flopsy, who is looking up at her. She pokes her tongue out at him and blows a raspberry. Although, that may have been a mistake. Flopsy repeatedly jumps from the springy bed up in the air, pawing at Pixel; Just missing her each time. She soars across the room like an arrow, slamming into the window face first. Pixel slides down the window, flopping onto the window ledge like a pancake. A disgruntled chime sounded as she fell, turning her glow red.

Flopsy looks over at Jasmine, hopping onto her chest while scratching his ear. He hops up to her as she's sleeping, sniffing her to make sure she's okay. Once convinced his owner was safe, he jumps onto her shoulder and curls up into a ball; Resting his head for the night.

SURGERY

J asmine awakes around half past six. Her mother quietly sob-
bing in the chair she had slept in. The tissue box still on
her bed from when Jasmine had to sneeze. Jasmine slowly sits
up, stretching out, sore from the uncomfortable sleeping posi-
tion. The tissues lift with Jasmine's hand gestures. She swipes her
fingers over to her mother who's looking upset. The tissues fly
through the air, landing perfectly on Avon's lap. She looks up and
smiles at Jasmine.

"Thank you, darling. But remember it's is not nice to throw
things." Avon said.

Jasmine rolls her eyes. "Sorry, mum." She was confused by how
adults could be so oblivious to her newfound skills.

Jasmine turns to see Flopsy at the top of the bed. She grabs him
and lays back down, resting her head on the pillow. Thoughts
of wonder were racing through Jasmine's head. It was difficult
to process what had happened the night before. Not quite sure
whether Pixel had just been a dream. The nurse wasn't a dream -
she had just moved levitating tissues without touching them. In
any case, Pixel, real or fake, seemed to fit in with last nights events
quite well.

"And besides, surely something would've happened to Flopsy if

Pixel was real. I sprayed pixie dust onto the poor thing." she continued to think. There was a sniffle in her ear. Sniff sniff. Sniff sniff sniff sniff. Jasmine tilts her head towards Flopsy. His nose twitched. He winked at Jasmine as she giggled.

"Did you sleep well, Flopsy?" Flopsy replies with a nod, followed by a sneeze. Glowing dust rushes from his nose, into the air, and instantly into Jasmine's, making her sneeze also.

"Do you need the tissues back, sweetheart?" Jasmine's mother asks, assuming both sneezes were from Jasmine.

"I'll be okay, thank you."

At that moment, the doctor who came in when Jasmine arrived walks through the door.

"Good morning, Jasmine!" He chirps. "Today, we're going to get you feeling better. How does that sound?" Jasmine doesn't say anything. It was time for the operation she needed. Fear started rushing through her body, making her hands shake and twitch.

"Don't worry! You'll be better before you know it." The doctor said, unlocking the wheels on the bed while another doctor starts to pull it away from the wall.

"We'll have to keep rabbit here, Or he might get messy." The doctor continues. Jasmine quickly grabs flopsy and holds him tight.

"Maybe it's best the rabbit stays on the bed," Avon suggests to the doctor, "At least until she's in the theatre."

"Okay, but it'll have to stay at the bottom of the bed..."

"He's a He." Jasmine interrupts. "Flopsy is a boy rabbit."

The doctor stares at Jasmine, stuttering. "Well, um, yes. Okay, He'll be safe at the bottom of the bed." Jasmine slowly lets Flopsy go. Avon takes Flopsy and places him at the bottom of the bed; Facing Jasmine.

The two doctors, followed by a couple of staff, move the bed out of the room. Jasmine lays back. All she could see were the lights and tiles of the ceiling - plus the occasional door frame. The walk to the theatre only took a couple of minutes. Above her, Jasmine could see a large lamp that was almost blinding her. The other doctor and the other staff locks the wheels on the bed in place and walks off. Nurses enter in blue aprons, masks and hats to assist the doctor.

"In a minute, Jasmine, you'll feel a little scratch in your arm. When you do, I want you to count back from 10 for me. Can you do that?" the doctor requests. Jasmine hesitates before giving a slight nod of agreement. She closes her eyes and tries to calm down. A figure began to stand over Jasmine, blocking out the light from the lamp. Jasmine opens her eyes. It was the ivory-skinned nurse from the evening before.

"Hey, little one. Don't be scared. Everything will be alright." The nurse whispers. Jasmine smiles, feeling more reassured. "Pixel is watching over you anyway, so you'll be better in no time." A sharp scratch in Jasmine's arm caught her attention. Time to count down.

10... 9... 8...

Jasmines eyes open. Many hours had passed. She was back in the hospital room. Unknown to Jasmine, she had been asleep for most of the day. Now it was nearly nightfall once again. The pains inside had disappeared, and she was feeling a lot better too!

"Leo, she's awake." Her mother's voice muttering from somewhere nearby. Jasmine slowly sits up in bed, her body aching as she starts to move. Her parents race over to hug her. Flopsy is also by her side. He gave a subtle smile that only Jasmine saw. Once the hugs had finished, Jasmine noticed another bed was also in the room now. In the bed sat a smaller boy with short dark hair.

"I'll go and get the doctor", Leo says, leaving the room. "We'll be back in a minute." Avon stands up to follow Leo out of the door. Jasmine looks at the other boy, who's amusing himself with an action figure. He looks up as the door slams shut.

"Hi," The little boy says. "I'm Theo."

"Hi, Theo. I'm Jasmine. It is nice to meet you." Jasmine replies with a big smile. "How old are you?"

"I'm five", Theo responds, throwing his action figure in the air.

"Ah. I'm six! Six and a half." There was a moment of silence. "Do you want to see something cool?"

Theo giggles and nods intently. Jasmine looks to the light switch and clicks her fingers. The lights flicker off. Jasmine clicks her fingers once more. The room lights up again, revealing a stunned five-year-old.

"Wow!" He shouts, not being able to shut his jaw through shock. His nose starts to twitch and sniffle. Jasmine looks at the box of tissues on the window ledge. She flicks her fingers and the tissues fly to Theo. Theo grabs a tissue and sneezes into it.

"How did you do that?" He asks excitedly, shocked by the magic.

"It's easy after a bit of practice." Jasmine says. "look at the box of tissues and tell it in your head to move. Then point to where you want it to go. Give it a go!" Theo tries to move the box. It doesn't move. Jasmine encourages Theo to try again. Theo looks intensely at the tissue box; Thinking very hard about it moving. He lifts his hand and swipes the air. The box still doesn't move.

"I can't do it!" Theo sighs, crossing his arm. "Yes, you can!" Jasmine replies. She smiles and looks out of the window. A warm glow protruding from the window ledge catches Jasmine's eye. Its Pixel waving and giggling; The sound of wind chimes whistled as she shook.

Jasmine looks back at Theo.

"You just need to believe!"

Printed in Great Britain
by Amazon

80367001R00016